Grandpa's
Indian Summer

JAMILA GAVIN

Grandpa's
Indian Summer

Illustrated by Mei-Yim Low

METHUEN CHILDREN'S BOOKS

BR(SC)
5f/c
C7070488 99

First published in Great Britain 1995
by Methuen Children's Books
an imprint of Reed Consumer Books Limited
Michelin House, 81 Fulham Road, London SW3 6RB
and Auckland, Melbourne, Singapore and Toronto

0 416 18965 2

A CIP catalogue record for this title
is available from the British Library

Printed and bound in Great Britain
by Bookcraft (Bath) Ltd.

Contents

1

Blood Relatives

It was dawn. Up on the flat roof of a house in Calcutta, Grandpa Chatterji sat cross-legged in a lotus position. Although his eyes were closed, inside his head he was watching. He could see his British grandchildren, Neetu and Sanjay excitedly getting ready to come to India to visit him. They dashed to and fro between an open suitcase and a bed full of presents which they were packing to bring to England.

Rahul climbed the stone steps up to the top, and as he stepped out on to the roof, the sun appeared, glinting between the flat leaves of the banana tree like a hard gold coin. He was carrying the photograph album. Quietly, he sat down next to his grandfather and crossed his legs.

'When my cousins come from England, will they bring me a present, Grandpa?' he whispered.

Grandpa smiled. 'What do you hope they will bring?'

'A cricketing outfit!' Rahul said without hesitation.

'Hmm,' murmured Grandpa. He knew his British grandson loved football. Yet maybe . . . Grandpa focused his mind . . .

Rahul opened the album and began to turn the pages. After a while he came to a section full of his British relatives in their English garden.

There was Sanjay in his football kit and there was Neeta in jeans and T-shirt playing on a

skateboard. 'They look very different from us. They don't look like my other cousins,' muttered Rahul.

'Hmmm,' Grandpa grunted thoughtfully. 'In some ways they are different; they wear different clothes, they eat different food and they play different games, but the same blood as yours flows through their veins.'

Rahul held up his hands and looked at the veins which spread like spidery veins in a leaf. How strange to think that people he had never seen, never touched, never ever spoken to, should have the same blood in their veins as he. He took his grandfather's old hand and held it up. He studied the thicker veins which criss-crossed like the spreading branches of a tree, from his knobbly knuckles to his great bony wrists.

'Your mother, and Neetu and Sanjay's mother are my daughters,' explained Grandpa Chatterji. 'They both have my blood in them, and so my blood is in you and your cousins too. We are blood relatives.'

'Blood relatives!' Rahul liked the sound of that. 'Is Vinod a blood relative?' He pointed to a photograph of a little boy standing in a family group at a wedding.

'No, he's just a relative,' said Grandpa. 'He

does not have any of our blood in his veins. He is a relative by marriage. He is your uncle's wife's sister's child!' And Grandpa burst out laughing when he saw Rahul's face screw up with puzzlement as if he were trying to work out a difficult sum. 'But what does it matter?' asked Grandpa, holding Rahul's smaller hand against his big old one. 'We're all part of the same blood of the universe. We all spring from God.'

However, for the rest of the day, Rahul went round trying to work out who was a blood relative and who a relative by marriage – and who were all the people he called aunts and uncles, when they weren't related at all, but just grown-up friends.

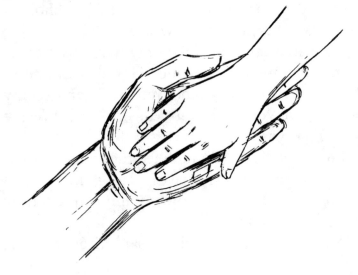

Across the ocean in England Mum said, 'What shall we take for Rahul and Radha?'

'If she's anything like me, then I think Radha would like a very complicated jigsaw puzzle,' said Neetu. 'The harder the better.'

'If he's anything like me, then I think we should take Rahul a football strip and scarf,' said Sanjay. 'He probably loves football.'

That night, Sanjay had a dream. He dreamt that he had arrived in Calcutta and Rahul came rushing up to him laughing. 'Did you bring me a cricketing outfit?' When Sanjay gave him a football strip instead, Rahul ran away shouting, 'I don't like football!'

Sanjay frowned in his sleep. 'How silly! Everyone loves football.'

Sanjay forgot all about his dream till he was in the sports shop with his mother, choosing a football strip for Rahul. They looked at all the colours. Should they take Manchester United, or Everton, or Liverpool or West Ham? He couldn't decide.

'You choose, Mum,' he muttered, suddenly losing interest. He wandered off round the shop. Suddenly he saw a picture of Ian Botham in full cricketing gear; pullover, helmet, gloves, knee-pads, bat and ball. Sanjay stood staring at it.

'Sanjay!' his mother called. 'I've decided on this football strip. Come and see. It's supposed to be a present from you.'

Sanjay didn't answer. He just stood in front of the cricketing picture like a statue.

'Sanjay! Have you gone to sleep?' laughed Mum.

'I had a dream,' murmured Sanjay. Suddenly it all started coming back to him. 'I dreamt that Rahul wanted a cricket outfit. He likes cricket, not football!'

Mum came and stood beside him. 'It's true, that Calcutta is cricket crazy. The whole of India is cricket crazy,' she said thoughtfully.

'Then we must buy him a cricket outfit, just like the one Ian Botham is wearing!' cried Sanjay waking up with a shout. 'I'm sure that's what he would like!'

Mum shrugged and went back to the shop assistant. 'I'm sorry,' she said. 'We've changed our minds. 'We'd like to buy a cricket kit: helmet, pullover, gloves, knee-pads, bat and ball.'

'I hope Radha likes her jigsaw puzzle. I didn't dream that she wanted anything else,' said Neetu.

The day arrived at last. The day Mum, Dad,

Neetu and Sanjay were setting off to visit Grandpa Chatterji in Calcutta.

Mum and Dad were concerned not to forget anything. They kept checking their list: passport, visas, tickets, malaria tablets, water-purifying tablets, tummy pills, mosquito repellent, insect-bite cream . . .

'We seem to be taking the whole chemist's shop,' Dad exclaimed.

'Better safe than sorry,' retorted Mum.

Then there were three suitcases: one for Mum and Dad: one for Neetu and Sanjay and one for the presents, including the jigsaw puzzle for Radha and the cricket kit for Rahul.

That morning, they had to get up very early. Everyone was rushing to and fro. Mr Bolton, their neighbour, had offered to drive them to the airport. They heard the beep of his car.

'Mr Bolton's here! Come on, everybody,' cried Dad.

Down came Mum and Dad's suitcase, down came Neetu and Sanjay's suitcase, and as Mum kept stuffing odds and ends into the hand luggage, Dad helped Mr Bolton stack the car.

Then they all piled in and, at last, they were off.

They had hardly settled down, when Dad began to check everything. 'Have we got the passports? Tickets and visas? Traveller's cheques . . .?'

They drove on a bit further, and Mum was thinking, 'Have we got everything? Malaria tablets, water tablets, mosquito repellent, insect-bite cream . . .'

Rahul sat cross-legged next to his grandfather. High in the sky, they saw a tiny silver speck etching a white line across the dawn sky. It was hard to believe that nearly three hundred people were flying through the air in that speck, which was really a jumbo jet.

'Soon Neetu and Sanjay will be up there,' murmured Grandpa Chatterji, happily.

'My blood relatives,' added Rahul happily, 'and I hope they don't forget to bring us presents.'

Grandpa closed his eyes.

* * *

'Did you pack my summer jacket?' asked Dad.

'Yes, but you nearly forgot your blue trousers. Luckily I remembered to get them from the dry cleaner's,' said Mum.

Then Neetu said, 'Have we got the suitcase with the presents?'

'I didn't put it in,' said Mum.

'I didn't put it in,' said Dad.

'I only stacked two suitcases on the roof rack,' said Mr Bolton.

'Oh no!' A terrible groan went up. 'We've forgotten the presents!'

With a jolt of brakes and a screech of tyres, Mr Bolton turned the car round, and they drove back home as fast as they could.

'That was a quick trip to India,' laughed the milkman from his milk float, as he hummed round the neighbourhood.

Dad found the third suitcase under Sanjay's bed. He heaved it on to the roof rack and tied it down. Then off they set again.

After a while, Mum said, 'Have we got everything?'

They went through the check list again: passport, tickets, traveller's cheques, malaria tablets, mosquito repellent . . . *three* suitcases.

* * *

'They won't forget the presents, will they, Grandpa?' asked Rahul.

'No,' smiled Grandpa, getting to his feet and stretching up as high as he could to the sky. Calcutta had woken up. The sounds of honking horns and beeping motor-scooters and roaring buses; cows cawing and imams calling to prayer reverberated all around them. 'No,' said Grandpa with certainty. 'They won't forget the presents.'

2

Where's Grandpa?

'Get up, get up, get up!' Aunty Meena rushed into the children's room. Radha and Rahul were still curled up tightly asleep.

'Come on, come on, come on!' Aunty Meena always liked to talk in threes.

Radha and Rahul groaned.

'Don't you want to be ready for your cousins? They're coming from England today so up, up, up! *Jangra bangra!* Have your baths, do your teeth, get dressed!'

Out in the courtyard, Great Grandma had already been moved into the soft early morning sun. She sat on her string bed covered with a quilt and reached out to give bits of carrot to her pet mynah bird, Hello. He was called Hello because when he first came, that was the only word he knew. Now, after living with the Chatterji family for a while, he knew lots of words and lots of voices, so that sometimes people didn't know whether it was a human speaking or the mynah bird.

Hello flew into the children's bedroom and settled on Radha's head. 'Get up, get up, get up!' he ordered in Aunty Meena's voice.

'Oh, shut up, Hello!' retorted Radha rudely.

'Shuttup, shuttup, shuttup!' repeated Hello.

Then Radha sat up with a jerk. 'Oh, Hello! You naughty boy. You've gone potty potty all over my hair,' and she dashed out of bed, rushed to the bathroom and tossed a jug of water over her head.

'Naughty boy, naughty boy, naughty boy!' agreed Hello.

Outside, the whole of Calcutta was up and about. What a sound of honking, tooting, cheeping, cawing, calling, singing and praying filled the air; and the shrill sound of reed pipes and thudding drums – for it was the season of weddings and processions; but it all seemed to be celebrating the arrival of their cousins from England.

Little Sassu who came to help round the house was already at the courtyard pump filling a pail. She had just turned up one day, asking if they needed help. Grandma Chatterji could see she was poor, so she said that Sassu could peel and chop vegetables, pick stones out of the lentils and sift the rice. But soon, Sassu showed she could do more: she washed the dishes, kneaded the *chapatti* dough and combed Great Grandma's hair. Once a month she would call her uncle from the gate. He was a rickshaw puller. Once a month she would sit like a lady, while her uncle pulled her all the way across the city to see her mother and father and all her brothers and sisters. She would give them her earnings, and then, after staying two nights, her uncle would pull her all the way back again.

'Sassu!' Radha was calling her.

'Sassu!' repeated Hello.

'Please come and plait my hair,' cried Radha.

Sassu came skipping over. She and Radha were friends and often played together.

The milkman called at the gate.

'*Korn?*' demanded Hello in Great Grandma's voice.

As '*Korn*' means 'Who is it?', the milkman called out, '*Doodwallah!* Milk!'

Grandma Chatterji had heard this conversation and bustled out to him carrying her milk pail. 'I'll need extra milk today,' she told him happily. 'My daughter and her family are visiting from England. They arrive today!'

The milkman lifted the huge churn of milk from his head and measured out a cataract of white milk into Grandma's pail.

'It's nearly time to go!' announced Uncle Ashok from the veranda. 'Where's Grandpa?'

'I don't know,' answered Radha, as Sassu oiled her hair till it shone inky black and then deftly divided and plaited it tightly, so that not one strand would stick out.

'I can't see him,' shouted Rahul from the roof where he had gone to fly his kite.

'He didn't come this way,' muttered Aunty Meena as she crouched over the beautiful welcoming *rangoli* pattern she was sprinkling outside the front gate.

'Heaven only knows where Grandpa is,' sighed Grandma Chatterji from the kitchen. She and Laxmi the cook were preparing a special spicy rice and lots of vegetables, ready for their hungry visitors from England.

'Grandpa!' squawked Hello, giving Great Grandma an affectionate nip on her ear.

'It's time to go!' insisted Uncle Ashok, getting agitated. 'Where is Grandpa? We'll be late if we don't leave now!'

They all crowded round the gate, trying not to step on Aunty Meena's *rangoli*. 'I'm gong to hail a taxi,' said Uncle Ashok, 'and if Grandpa doesn't turn up, we'll just have to leave without him.'

He stood on the edge of the pavement, just between the *paan* seller and the pavement barber. Cars and cows and buses and rickshaws all rushed by, but he couldn't see a yellow Hindustan taxi. He looked at his watch and began to feel nervous. 'We're going to be late,' fretted Uncle Ashok. 'I can't see a taxi anywhere. How is it you can never get one when you really need it?'

'I see one!' shouted Rahul.

'Get it, get it, get it!' cried Aunty Meena.

'There's already someone in it,' groaned Uncle Ashok.

'Perhaps it will stop here,' said Radha. 'It's coming this way.'

The yellow taxi came nearer and nearer.

'Taxi, taxi!' yelled the mynah bird.

They couldn't see who was in the taxi. All they could see were flowers.

Then suddenly, a voice rang out, 'Come on, all of you! Get in. We're going to be late!'

'Grandpa!' everyone shouted.

They all piled in, trying not to squash the garlands of marigolds and jasmine and bunches of carnations and lilies.

'Why did you disappear just at the time we had to go?' grumbled Uncle Ashok.

'I had to go to the flower market. We couldn't

greet our guests without flowers!' said Grandpa Chatterji. 'And anyway, I knew there would be taxis to be found there.

It was very crowded at the airport and they had to wait such a long time. As passengers began coming out with all their bags and suitcases, Radha and Rahul looked and looked to see if they could recognise their cousins, as they had only ever seen them in photographs. Then, suddenly, there was a family who looked Indian, but who wore western clothes. The girl and boy were both wearing jeans and trainers and carried sports bags on their shoulders.

'Didi, Didi, Didi!' cried Aunty Meena, rushing towards her older sister. Then what a lot of hugging and kissing and a fierce pinching of cheeks there was. Neetu and Sanjay's mother and father both bent down respectfully and touched the feet of Grandpa and Grandma Chatterji.

'Welcome to Calcutta!' beamed Grandpa, draping their necks with garlands, and thrusting bunches of roses and lilies into his daughter's arms.

Grandpa wanted them all to squeeze into one taxi. He couldn't bear to be parted from any of them, but finally he agreed, two taxis were necessary.

'This is better than Disneyland,' exclaimed Neetu and Sanjay, as the taxis drove at breakneck speed, weaving in and out of the traffic and swerving to avoid cows and dogs and pigs who wandered into the road.

Suddenly, Neetu and Sanjay's taxi began to make funny noises. It began to cough and choke and splutter. It went slower and slower and finally stopped – right in the middle of the road. Horns were hooting and honking: 'Get out of the way!' – but what were they to do?

'I'm sorry,' said the taxi driver. 'My taxi's broken down. It won't go any further. You'll have to find another one.'

'We can all squeeze in with the others,' declared Grandpa Chatterji.

'No – we can't,' groaned Uncle Ashok, but though they stood and stood and waved their arms, another taxi didn't come along.

'We'll have to try and squeeze in,' persisted Grandpa Chatterji. 'We can't stand here all day.'

Then over the roar of the traffic, they heard a little voice calling! 'Radha! Rahul! Are those your cousins arrived from England?'

There, being pulled along by her uncle, was Sassu in a rickshaw.

'I've got a good idea!' exclaimed Grandpa Chatterji rushing over to have a word with Sassu's uncle.

Great Grandma sat on her string bed in the courtyard, listening. She too was full of excitement that her grandchild and great-grandchildren were coming. Her eyes were very bad now, but her ears were sharp. She listened to the sounds in the street outside. She could hear the hawkers shouting their wares, the tring-tring of bicycle bells, dogs barking, crows cawing and the roar of traffic. But her ear was tuned to pick up the sound of an arrival.

She didn't stir when she heard a taxi drawing

up. She didn't move when she heard the voices of excited children thanking Sassu and her uncle for pulling them all the way home in his rickshaw. She just waited patiently, stroking with one finger the sleek black feathers of her pet bird.

Suddenly, Hello hopped excitedly and called out in Great Grandma's voice, '*Korn?*'

Great Grandma looked up. 'Who is it?' she whispered.

Neetu and Sanjay came forward shyly. They touched her feet and embraced her. 'Great Grandma, it's us!'

3

Calcutta Night

Neetu awoke. It was a dark, dark night. She knew she should be asleep, but her body wanted to be awake. Her body thought it was eight o'clock in the morning and time to get up. But her body hadn't yet understood that it was no longer in England; it was in India, and the time was only three o'clock in the morning.

Suddenly her brain was pounding with images and new experiences. She smiled when she remembered how Grandpa Chatterji had introduced them to their cousins, Radha and Rahul.

'Are they blood relatives?' Rahul had demanded.

'The same blood which flows in my veins and your veins also flows in theirs,' Grandpa had answered, and they examined each others hands and then studied each other's faces to see what other things were the same.

'Do you like cricket?' Rahul asked Sanjay.

'Well . . . I prefer football.' Then when he saw Rahul's face drop with disappointment, Sanjay cried, 'but look what we've brought for you!' and he excitedly unpacked the cricket outfit.

'Do you like jigsaws and flying kites?' Radha asked Neetu.

'I've never flown a kite,' said Neetu, 'but look what I've brought for you!' and she gave Radha the very complicated jigsaw with a picture of Big Ben and the Houses of Parliament.

At first, Neetu thought she would be afraid of Grandma Chatterji. Grandma didn't smile as much as Grandpa and she had very piercing, light brown eyes which looked as if they could read your mind. But suddenly, Grandma said softly, 'Here, little granddaughter, here is something for you,' and she slipped into Neetu's hand a little cloth bag, which drew open and closed with a twisty cord and was all stitched with silver threads and mirrors. Inside were ten rupees.

Neetu breathed deeply in and out. Now she was really awake. She could smell the garland of fresh marigolds which Grandpa Chatterji had draped round her neck at the airport. She hadn't

taken it off for the rest of the day, and before getting into bed, she had hung it on the bedpost near her head. Its perfume mingled with the sweet lotus scent of the incense sticks which burned in the *puja* room.

The *puja* room. Neetu shivered with awe as she thought of the strange inhabitants in that room. Three small figures dressed in silks and adorned with tiny garlands of jasmine and rosebuds stood on an altar. The figures were gods: there was the goddess Laxmi, who was the bringer of good fortune, the elephant-headed god Ganesh, who was the bringer of wisdom and the remover of obstacles, and there was the dancing figure of Lord Shiva, the destroyer of all evil. On a wall

31

was a gold-framed picture, also garlanded. It was a picture of Rama and Sita – the god prince and goddess princess who had fought such battles with Ravanna, the king of the demons. But it was as though the gods were alive. The family dressed them, fed them and cared for them and, every day, they prayed to them. Before supper that night, Radha showed Neetu how they took a little bit of food from every dish and placed it before the gods in the *puja* room. 'Feed God then feed self,' she told her.

As Neetu lay in her bed, she wondered if those statues came alive; if Shiva danced through the darkness, waving his six arms and killing demons; if Laxmi smiled at what a beautiful *rangoli* pattern Aunty Meena had made, to please her, as well as the relatives from England, and if good, wise Ganesh waved away troubles with his long trunk.

How strange, Neetu thought, as she lay there

in her Indian bed, even in the middle of the night, there is no silence. The air seemed to be throbbing with muffled drums and tinkling bells. Somewhere out there a dog was barking and she wondered why; somewhere out there a man was singing, soft and low, and voices mumbled in prayer. Up in the highest branches of a neem tree, a restless bird squawked sleepily, and Neetu wondered whether birds dream too.

'Neetu!' called Sanjay in a sad, small voice. 'I want to go home.'

'Why, Sanjay?'

'I don't like India. I don't like the smell and it's too noisy.'

Before she could say anything, they heard another sound. It was very close. Neetu sat up, and saw a gleam of light coming from beyond the veranda. She heard the squeal of the pump and the whoosh of water. She slid out of bed and fumbled for her slippers. Sanjay was already sitting, his eyes shining across the room like two moons.

'Where are you going?' he whispered.

'Just to see,' answered Neetu.

'I'm coming too,' muttered Sanjay.

Their feet made no sound on the cool, stone floor as they crossed their room and silently pushed open the door.

Who was that bending over the pump? The moon sparkled silver on the rush of water that flooded out and was tossed over a gleaming body. A cupped hand filled with liquid and a face bent to drink. They heard the water rattle round in the cheeks; another sip and they heard gargling and rinsing and the sound of murmured prayers. Then a jug was lifted, and a cataract of water was poured all over the head. As a towel rubbed the hair and a face finally turned towards them, they saw – it was Grandpa Chatterji.

'What are you doing, Grandpa?' whispered Neetu.

'I'm praying,' answered Grandpa.

'I thought you were washing,' grunted Sanjay.

'Washing is praying,' replied Grandpa with a smile. 'Now I'm going up on the roof to do my exercises, will you come or will you sleep?'

'We'll come,' said Neetu and Sanjay both together.

They climbed the stone steps which curled round from the courtyard and went up on to the flat stone roof with a balustrade all around. They ducked between the criss-cross of washing lines, and passed the television aerial with the paper kite stuck in its prongs, and went round to where they could look across the city all the way to the river, coiling and glinting like a great serpent.

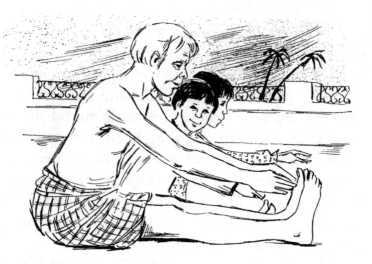

First they did stretching and bending, touching
their toes and their heads to their knees and their
knees to their chins and then Grandpa pulled
some dry towels off the washing line and they lay
down on their backs. They lifted each leg and
rotated each ankle, pointed their toes up to the
stars and bent their knees to touch their noses.

'Be a cobra,' said Grandpa, and they rolled on
to their tummies and raised their heads right up.

'Be a bow,' said Grandpa, and they curved their
bodies and stretched their muscles as if you could
shoot arrows from it.

'Be a camel,' said Grandpa, and they knelt with
arms in front and arched their backs like camel's
humps.

'Now I'm going to be a lotus and meditate,' said Grandpa, and they copied him as he sat cross-legged with straight back and hands hung loosely over his knees, and they breathed deeply in and out, in and out . . .

'I feel sleepy,' whispered Sanjay.

'So do I,' nodded Neetu.

They turned to Grandpa, but didn't speak, because he looked as if he had floated away. So they left him. Quietly, they got to their feet and tiptoed across the roof, down the stairs and back to their room.

'Tomorrow, I'm going to play cricket with Rahul,' whispered Sanjay, 'though I wish he'd play football.'

'Tomorrow, I'm going to the kite shop with Radha and we're going to fly kites up on the roof,' said Neetu, 'and we'll see whose kite can fly the highest.'

There was silence. Then Sanjay whispered, 'Neetu, are you awake?'

'No,' came a muffled voice.

'I think I may like India after all.'

'Good,' murmured Neetu and, as if they lay within the petals of a lily, they drifted away into sleep once more.

4

The Cricket Match

'Rahul! Cricket!' the voices called from outside.

'Rahul! Cricket!' repeated Hello, the mynah bird.

Rahul leapt to his feet. He could never say no to a game of cricket.

'Come on, Sanjay, you must play too!'

'I don't play cricket,' shrugged Sanjay. 'I only play football,' and how he wished there was a football around for him to kick.

'Go out and tell them I'm coming in a minute,' cried Rahul, rushing off to his room.

Sanjay wandered out of the gate. Where could they play cricket, anyway? he wondered. Here they were in the middle of the city, and he hadn't noticed any parks or open spaces. He looked up and down the busy road, but couldn't see Rahul's friends.

Then Grandpa Chatterji called out, 'They're in the lane! I'll show you!' The truth was, Grandpa Chatterji loved cricket too, and was always trying to join in. He took Sanjay's hand and led him between the meandering cows and the tinkling bicycles and the hooting, tooting cars and auto-rickshaws and turned the corner into the lane which ran down the side of the house.

'Where's Rahul?' cried the boys. Two or three of them were crouched over some sticks which they were propping up between tin cans.

'He's coming,' answered Sanjay.

When the boys had set their bails, they began to discuss who should bat and bowl first.

'Let me start the batting!' demanded Grandpa,

snatching up a rough piece of wood which had been hacked out to resemble a cricket bat.

The boys grinned. They always let Grandpa Chatterji play for a short while.

'Football's got nothing on cricket,' Grandpa told Sanjay with a wicked smile as he positioned himself in front of the bails. 'Cricket is the best game in the world. I'll make sure you can play it before you go back. Now watch me! Who's bowling?' he called.

A boy called Ashkan tossed an old rubber ball into the air and took up a bowling position while the others rushed to be fielders.

'Hey, Sanjay!' they shouted. 'Stand over there and be an extra till you know how to play.'

Grandpa wriggled his body expectantly and held the bat in front of him, watching the bowler. Ashkan swayed for a moment – to and fro . . . to and fro . . . as if measuring every step. Then he broke into a short run, swung his arm over his head and – pow! The ball hit the bat with a wham and it flew up into the sky.

'Catch, catch, catch!' cried the fielders, rushing towards it with faces upturned. 'Oh!' A groan went up as Tarun, who ran as fast as he could, missed the catch and had to run right out into the road with the cyclists weaving round him and cows blocking his way and the auto-rickshaws tooting and the shopkeepers yelling to tell him where the ball had rolled.

Meanwhile, Grandpa had set off, trying to get in as many runs as he could, and by the time Tarun returned and tossed the ball to Ashkan, Grandpa Chatterji was on his fourth run.

Suddenly Ashkan shouted excitedly. 'Just take a look at Rahul!'

'Wow! He looks like Kapil Dev himself!' the boys exclaimed with awe.

Rahul came striding down the lane – somewhat awkwardly, as he wasn't used to wearing leg-pads, or a helmet or large white padded gloves. In one hand, he brandished a brand-new cricket bat, while in the other was a shiny red-leather cricket ball – the real thing, with white stitching.

The boys clustered round him as if he were a god. With tender hands, they touched his helmet and pads and grasped his gloved hands in theirs. They took it in turns to hold the bat – so shining and oil-bright, and how lovingly they rolled the ball in their hands and tossed it gently into the air, fearing to be the first to drop it and get it all dusty.

'Where did you get this?' they cried with wonderment.

'England!' replied Rahul proudly. 'Sanjay brought it for me from England.'

They all turned and looked at Sanjay, who beamed with pleasure.

'Now I expect you to play like a professional,' said Grandpa, wagging his finger, and he hobbled off to have a rest after all his exertions.

'And look what else I have!' cried Rahul. From under his arm, he extricated three wooden stumps and two bails to go on top. It was the real thing. With whoops of joy, they were snatched from his hands. The tin cans and bits of wood were kicked away into the ditch and the new stumps were carefully propped and wedged with bricks so that they stood upright and the bails balanced on top.

Rahul proudly took his position as batsman and Tarun prepared to bowl the first ball. He set off running, then swung his arm round and up and over. The ball left his hand like a loosed bird, soaring in the air. Rahul kept his eye on it as it hurtled towards him. He swung the bat and – *thwack* – the ball was struck and flew back into the air and the fielders scattered.

All afternoon they played, Rahul allowing each of his friends to use his new kit. Whenever a boy took up the shiny bat and put on the leg-pads and helmet, he felt like Kapil Dev out there on Eden Cricket Ground in Calcutta. He could imagine himself surrounded by thousands of people who had crammed into the ground to see the match; or eagerly peered at by thousands more who couldn't get in, but had climbed up trees and telegraph poles, or begged their way into high windows which overlooked the ground. And when he held the bat, wagging it in front of him, trying to assess at what speed and pace the ball would be bowled to him – it was Imran Khan he imagined facing him, menacingly rubbing every scrap of dust off the ball against his trouser leg.

The bails, balanced on those clean, new stumps, hadn't fallen yet. Then Rahul bowled to Ashkan. Rahul fixed his eye on the stumps. He set off running fast; Ashkan braced himself for a fast spin, but at the last moment, Rahul cunningly changed pace and threw the ball in a wide arc. Ashkan was caught by surprise and the ball spun past him and struck down the stumps and the bails as if they were skittles.

'Yeah!' everyone cheered. Grandpa Chatterji, watching from the veranda, couldn't sit back any longer. He had regained his breath and was ready for more. He longed to try the new bat. He came

leaping out into the lane. 'You don't mind if I just
try out the bat, do you?'

'You'd better put on the knee-pads and helmet
as well, Grandpa,' laughed Rahul.

Grandpa Chatterji feels like a young boy again.
As he stands in front of the wicket, he is back
once more in his school's cricket eleven, but he
pretends he's playing for Calcutta at Eden
Garden. It is an important match. There is a
breathless hush. Everyone is depending on him.
They need eight more runs to win. Can he pull it
off? He taps the ground before him and nervously
adjusts the bat in his hands. Then he fixes his eye
on the ball. It is not Rahul standing before him
ready to bowl, but the great Sunil Gavaskar. A

45

figure is bounding towards him. With what grace his arm goes back and round and over. The red ball comes spinning through the air. But it can't escape his eye. He swings the bat with a rapid swipe and strikes the ball with all his might. The sound of leather on willow echoes all around. A gasp goes up from the boys, but to Grandpa Chatterji, it sounds like the gasp from fifteen thousand people – no – from the whole of India, whose ears are glued to radios, and eyes to television. The nation comes to a standstill and holds its breath.

He sets off running. He'll easily get those runs and his team will win. Strange. The yells of triumph have turned to groans of despair.

'Oh no! Now you've gone and done it, Grandpa!' wailed Rahul.

The red leather ball had sailed far over their upstretched hands; far over the road, honking with traffic; far over the stalls of the astonished shop-keepers; over a far distant wall it went and out of sight.

The boys chased after it. They tried to climb the wall – balancing on shoulders and heaving each other up – but it was too high. Groaning with dejection, they gave up and went home. They all knew whose house it had fallen into. Dr

46

Ranjit Bose was the grumpiest man in Calcutta. He was always chasing off the boys. He would never give them back the ball.

Rahul didn't say a word, but went silently to his room. Sanjay went over to sit with Great Grandma and chat to Hello. Grandpa Chatterji took himself off to the veranda and sat cross-legged on his mat. He closed his eyes and breathed deeply. Into his brain, came the image of a shiny, round red-leather cricket ball with white stitching.

At tea-time, Rahul was still too upset to speak and he wouldn't sit next to his grandfather.

'Don't be too upset, Rahul,' Neetu tried to comfort him. 'We'll send you another ball from England.'

'How can you?' grunted Rahul dejectedly.

'You can't just post a cricket ball.'

'Someone may find it and return it to you,' suggested Grandpa gently. 'You never know.'

'I know,' declared Rahul, scornfully. 'Who would return such a ball if they found it? Especially not Dr Bose.'

'We'll see,' murmured Grandpa Chatterji.

When Grandma saw all those long faces, she brought out her cakes – even though they were really meant for Sunday tea. She knew a tragedy had befallen them.

Suddenly, a shadow, no thicker than a toothpick, fell across the dorrway.

'*Korn?*' demanded Hello in Great Grandma's voice.

There stood a thin, gangly, bony boy in grey school shorts and white shirt, looking very awkward and shy.

'Come in, come in, come in!' urged Aunty Meena kindly.

The boy slipped off his sandals and stepped inside.

'Can we help you?' asked Grandpa, as the boy seemed very tongue-tied.

'My grandfather . . . Dr Bose . . .'

There was an intake of breath from everyone.

'My grandfather asks if any of you lost a

cricket ball this morning?' I asked round the district and the shopkeepers sent me here.'

'I lost a cricket ball!' shouted Rahul excitedly. 'A brand-new, shiny, red-leather cricket ball, all the way from England.'

'My grandfather would like you to call and collect it,' the boy stammered. 'Can you come with me, now?'

Rahul looked at his grandfather with alarm. What, go to Dr Bose's house and risk getting his ears boxed? 'Can't you go, Grandpa?' he begged.

'Go, Rahul. Go with the boy,' said Grandpa reassuringly. 'You see. It will be all right. I know it will.'

So Rahul put on his shoes and went with the boy to the house of Dr Bose.

It was a great, crumbling, old-style house, with lots of shuttered windows and balconies overflowing with flowerpots and creepers. He followed the boy up long, stone veranda steps, through shadowed arches and into a darkened living room.

'*Korn?*' asked a gruff old man's voice from within the depths of a deep armchair.

'It's me, Grandfather, Amu. I've found the owner of the cricket ball.'

'Let me see him then,' and a thin, gnarled hand waved them before him.

Rahul edged round the chair to face Dr Bose, but stood at a safe distance, out of reach.

'Come closer, boy, stand where I ccan see you properly,' the old man croaked impatiently.

Rahul came forward and stood directly in front. He had never really looked at Dr Bose before. Now he saw an aged face, creased with pain, but with eagle-sharp eyes which peered up at him from behind steel-rimmed spectacles.

'Who hit the ball into my garden? Was it you?'

'No, sir, not exactly . . .' stammered Rahul.

'Not exactly? What is this – not exactly? Did you or didn't you?'

'I bowled the ball, sir, but my grandfather batted it. He got a bit carried away because it is a

real cricket ball from England,' explained Rahul apologetically.

'Is this the ball?' The old man held up a red-leather cricket ball.

'Yes, sir, that's mine!' Rahul stared longingly at the ball. He wanted to grab it and run away from this sad, gloomy house.

'I'll give you back your ball but only in exchange for a favour,' said the old man.

Rahul waited respectfully, wondering what possible favour he could do for Dr Bose.

'This is my grandson, Amar. Come here, Amu, stand where I can see you!' he commanded.

The bony boy shuffled round and stood next to Rahul. Rahul glanced at him and realised that they were both about the same age.

'Amar is down from boarding school to stay

with me for the holidays. It's lonely for him, stuck with a decrepit old man like me. So, in exchange for returning your cricket ball, will you allow Amar to play cricket with you?'

'Of course, sir, of course!' cried Rahul with relief. 'Come any time you like! We're always playing,' he told the boy.

Amu's face broke into a wide-open smile.

As Amu was leading Rahul away, Dr Bose suddenly called out, 'By the way, that grandfather of yours is quite a cricketer. He must have given that ball a terrific swipe for it to reach my garden. Send him my congratulations, will you?'

'Oh yes, sir! Indeed, sir!' laughed Rahul.

The next day the boys were out again in the lane. They propped up the stumps and bails with the bricks and picked the fielders and the batsmen. Rahul stood at the wicket in all his gear. He held the bat expectantly, becoming Kapil Dev again in his mind's eye. Amar faced him as the bowler. Rahul's friends felt a bit nervous about having Dr Bose's grandson to play – especially as he didn't look as if he could swat a fly, let alone play cricket. He held the ball in his hand, then rubbed it against his shorts. Nervously, he clenched and unclenched his knobbly knees, then with a nod at

Rahul, he began his run. His charge was swift and surprising. His arm whirled round and he let loose a deceptive fast ball. It flew through the air and skidded on the loose dust, homing in on the stumps. Rahul instinctively got down to it and lifted the ball with the meat of the bat. THWACK. The ball seemed to balloon out. It soared out over the mid-on and over all the fielders running with their arms outstretched. It began to fall exactly over Sanjay, who had been standing in again at extra cover.

'Catch it, catch it, catch it!' the voices shrieked.

For an instant, Sanjay was bewildered. Then he heard Grandpa Chatterji's voice shouting, 'Sanjay! Look at the ball! Put up your arms, open your hands!'

Sanjay looked up and saw the ball plummeting down on him. He held up his arms and opened his hands. Plop! The ball dropped straight into his fingers. Its force threw him to the ground, but he didn't let go. He rolled over with the ball clutched to his chest, while everyone rushed around him.

'Well done, Sanjay!' they yelled, and lifted him up on to their shoulders as if he were a hero.

On the other side of the street, two old men watched the game from a tea shop.

'They're not too bad, those grandsons of ours,

eh?' Dr Bose's eyes twinkled as he poured Grandpa Chatterji another cup of tea.

That night, before dropping off to sleep, Sanjay asked his dad, 'Do you think I could have a cricket kit for my next birthday?'

Dad grinned with pleasure. 'I'll speak to Mum about it.'

5

Grandma's Cakes

All around the house came the sound of children's voices. They were playing hide-and-seek. Everyone joined in. They raced in and out of the rooms, across the courtyard, up the stone steps on to the roof, down again, on to the veranda and out into the garden. Their voices rose as they counted, yelled, giggled, snuffled and shuffled into their hiding places, shushing each other up and stifling their laughter. Then there would be a brief silence while the seeker went seeking.

Sassu was hiding her eyes and counting. Neetu looked unsure of where to hide, but Radha grabbed her arm and said, 'Come with me! I'll show you a good place.' Everyone scuttled off in all directions.

A wonderful warm smell was wafting through

the house. It followed the children wherever they went. There was no hiding place where the delicious sweet aroma didn't reach and make them smack their lips.

'What's that nice smell?' whispered Neetu, as she crouched next to Radha in their hiding place behind the wardrobe.

'Is today Friday?' asked Radha. 'Then it's Grandma's baking day.'

They heard Sassu shout, 'Coming!' and saw her rush past. They heard her stop at the kitchen to see if anyone was hiding there, and then carry on up to the roof.

Radha and Neetu crept out. 'Sassu's checked the kitchen and she won't come back. Let's see if

Grandma needs help with her cakes.'

Grandma Chatterji stood there with a large mixing bowl in her arms, stirring and stirring – flour, butter, eggs, milk, sugar, nuts and raisins. Her oven was already hot and glowing with one batch of cakes. Now she began to spoon out her mixture on to a cupped tray for another batch.

Radha and Neetu appeared in the doorway. 'Can we help with the cakes?' asked Radha coming up to the mixing bowl and dipping in a finger.

'*Arreh!* Don't go poking your fingers in my bowl!' snapped Grandma sternly. Aren't you meant to be hiding?'

Neetu felt a little afraid of Grandma because she could look so fierce. She seemed to make the rules in the house and everyone obeyed her. Neetu shyly tugged Radha's hand and whispered, 'We'd better go back to our hiding place before Sassu finds us.'

But Radha wasn't afraid. She circled Grandma, scooping up bits of cake mixture with her little finger.

'Stop it, Radha!' Grandma ordered and smacked her granddaughter's hand. 'She's such a naughty girl – don't you think so, Neetu? She's as bad as the sparrows.

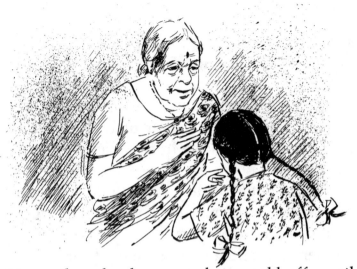

Neetu thought they were being told off, until she saw Grandma's light brown eyes – which could be as hard as walnuts – sparkling with friendliness. Grandma finished spooning out the mixture on to the tray, and then, to their joy, offered them the bowl and spoon to lick.

Suddenly, a cluster of sparrows hurtled in through the fretwork which criss-crossed the open kitchen window. Chirruping excitedly in hectic play, they darted and dived among the kitchen shelves.

'Arreh, these sparrows! They're such a nuisance. They do potty potty all over the place! Grandpa wants to put a wire mesh over the windows, but I won't let him. A wire mesh may stop the sparrows, but it would make my kitchen so hot in the summer, that I wouldn't need to use my oven for baking. So, what to do?' sighed Grandma.

The girls ducked as the sparrows zoomed round, weaving in and out of each other, then they dived through the fretwork and out into the garden again.

'Well, I suppose they are all God's creatures,' murmured Grandma, 'and have as many rights as we do. So, we'll let them be.'

There was still a lot of cake mixture left round the sides of the bowl when they heard footsteps coming.

'Quick! Sassu's coming!' exclaimed Radha. 'We'd better hide,' and she dragged Neetu away back to their hiding place behind the wardrobe.

But it wasn't Sassu. It was Sanjay who appeared in the doorway, his mouth watering with the smell of the baking cakes.

'Hello, Sanjay!' said Grandma. 'Aren't you meant to be hiding?'

'I don't know a good place,' complained Sanjay, his eyes on the bowl and spoon which were still thick with cake mixture. 'Hmmm!' He slid a finger round the inside of the mixing bowl. 'Are these cakes for us?' he asked, fervently sucking his finger.

'Yes,' said Grandma, taking one batch out of the oven and putting in another.

Sanjay's hand stretched out hopefully, but Grandma flicked it away with a frown. 'No, Sanjay. These are for tea on Sunday,' and she looked so severe, that Sanjay didn't dare beg to let him have just one! 'But here, child,' she said with a sudden glinting smile, 'you can lick the spoon if you like.'

Sanjay eagerly snatched the spoon she offered and began to lick it all over: up the stem, round the neck, and he was just getting to the really thick bit on the head, when suddenly Sassu appeared and grabbed him. 'I've caught Sanjay! Now it's his turn to hide his eyes.'

'That's not fair,' moaned Sanjay. 'I wasn't even hiding!'

'Well, you should have been!' cried Sassu unmercifully.

The other children appeared flushed and laughing. They made Sanjay stand by a veranda pillar and hide his eyes. 'No peeping,' Rahul warned him. 'And be sure to count to a hundred!'

'Sanjay can't count to a hundred!' scoffed Neetu.

'Oh yes, I can!' retorted Sanjay and began chanting loudly: one . . . two . . . three . . .

The children scattered. Sanjay did get stuck around fifteen, so he went back to the beginning and started again, getting quieter and quieter till be was murmuring softly and waiting a long enough time so that it would seem as though he had counted to a hundred. Then he yelled, 'COMING!'

'COMING!' echoed Hello from out in the courtyard, and burst out cackling.

Sanjay wandered about from room to room; he looked under beds, behind chairs and sofas; he tugged at curtains in case someone was coiled up inside them and climbed up on to the roof to search among the washing lines flapping with clothes. But his heart wasn't really in it. He couldn't stop thinking about Grandma's cakes. He went back to the kitchen, but the bowl and spoon had been cleared away. Grandma had finished her baking and gone to wash her hair under the courtyard tap. He lingered, held by the rich warm smell, and wondered where Grandma had stored her cakes. He looked around, pretending he was hunting for the others. Perhaps someone was hiding under the table or in the cupboard.

Suddenly, he saw a movement behind a far curtain. He dashed over and flung it aside.

'Caught you!' he shouted triumphantly.

'Sssh!' It was Grandpa Chatterji, looking extremely guilty, with a cake clutched in his fingers. Behind the curtain was a small pantry, and standing in a corner was a metal chest. 'I was just checking to see if Grandma's cakes were up to her usual standard,' he exclaimed with a smile like a wicked robber. 'Aren't you meant to be looking for everyone! Go on! Be off with you! There's no one hiding here.' Grandpa Chatterji drew aside the curtain and bustled Sanjay out of the kitchen. 'Now I must get along to the post office.' And Grandpa Chatterji hurried away.

Sanjay couldn't help himself; he went back into the kitchen. A sparrow flew in through the window and darted behind the curtain into the

pantry. Sanjay followed. The sparrow chirruped on the ledge above the tin chest and cocked his head sideways, looking with an eager eye. A rich warm sugary smell hung in the air. Sanjay lifted the lid. There were the newly baked cakes, stored like gold. There were several layers all lined up on their trays, with clean white napkins in between.

'I wonder if Grandma's cakes are up to standard?' said Sanjay to himself. He bent down and sniffed and before he knew it, he had stuffed one cake into his mouth and swallowed it.

'That one seems to be up to standard,' he murmured, brushing away the crumbs from his chin. The sparrow flew down quickly to peck as a large black ant peered out of a crack in the wall. 'I wonder if they are all as good as that.'

The sparrow spun in the air expectantly. Sanjay wriggled a hand down the side. There were many layers of cakes. Perhaps he should check one cake from each layer. He lifted out another.

Puzzled voices were ringing round the house. 'Sanjay! Come and find me!' Gradually, it began to dawn on those who were hiding, that Sanjay wasn't looking for them. They came out feeling annoyed. 'Sanjay! Where are you?' shouted Rahul. 'If you don't play properly, we won't let you join in our games!'

But there was no sign of Sanjay. Now everyone was looking for him. Inside and outside and up on the roof and all round the garden. They even looked in the lane outside the house, calling and calling his name.

The grown-ups were consulted. 'Have you seen Sanjay?' they asked Grandma Chatterji, who was drying her hair in the sun.

'Have you seen Sanjay?' they asked Aunty Meena who was shelling peas on the veranda.

'Have you seen Sanjay?' they whispered to Great Grandma Chatterji. But she was dozing, and Hello called out, 'Sanjay! Naughty boy, naughty boy!'

Grandpa Chatterji came walking back from the post office. 'We've lost Sanjay. Is he with you?' they asked.

'No . . .' Grandpa looked thoughtful.

Suddenly Grandma shouted, '*Arreh!* Look at all those ants coming from my kitchen!'

A long, long trail of large, shining black ants came out of the kitchen, across the veranda, down the steps and trooped out into the garden.

'Look, look, look! They're carrying

something,' exclaimed Aunty Meena.

Everyone bent down to look. 'Cake crumbs!' cried Grandma. 'Has someone been eating my cakes?'

The sight of all those ants made Neetu's skin prickle, but she couldn't help being fascinated by the busy, determined creatures, moving to and fro in a constantly flowing line, as they shunted cake crumbs from one to another.

'I hope they haven't got at Grandma's cakes,' muttered Radha.

Grandma Chatterji looked accusingly at Grandpa Chatterji. 'Have you been at my cakes again?' she demanded sternly. She knew what a weakness Grandpa had for her cakes.

Before Grandpa could reply, they all heard a faint whimpering. They hurried into the kitchen. The train of ants crossed the floor and disappeared behind the curtain. Radha ran over and flung the curtain aside and Neetu gave a shriek of horror. There stood Sanjay on top of the tin chest with a cake in each hand. Crumbs and tears dripped from his cheeks. He was surrounded by a vast sea of black ants.

'Silly India, silly India,' he whimpered.

Grandpa Chatterji plunged through the swarming creatures and held open his arms.

Sanjay leapt into them gratefully, whispering, 'I'm sorry, I'm sorry, I'm sorry!'

'Oh, Sanjay!' cried Neetu. 'You naughty boy. You've been stealing Grandma's cakes.'

'Don't blame Sanjay,' Grandma said sternly. 'He learned it from someone who should have known better!' and she wagged her finger at Grandpa Chatterji. 'No cakes for you this week!' she said.

Grandpa Chatterji bowed his head. 'Sorry!'

'Sorree,' squawked Hello, solemnly.

The children all burst out laughing. 'Sanjay had such a good hiding place, no one would have found him if it hadn't been for the ants!' they shouted, then like a flock of sparrows, rushed off again to play.

Grandpa beckoned Sanjay and whispered in his ear, 'In India, food is very precious. Nothing goes to waste. If you drop one crumb, there is always a pig, a dog, a monkey, a cockroach, a sparrow or an ant to come and eat it up. So next time, be sure not to drop a single crumb.'

Sanjay nodded, then whispered back, 'Grandpa, can you show me another good hiding place?'

The River

'Before you go home to England, you must bathe in the river. Today, we are going to take Great Grandma Chatterji for her bathe, so you can go too,' said Grandpa Chatterji.

Neetu and Sanjay were amazed. Why, Great Grandma even had to be helped to the pump in the courtyard. How could she want to go to the river to bathe?

But no one seemed surprised.

Great Grandma liked to go in a horse-drawn carriage, so that afternoon Uncle Ashok set off to find one. Soon he returned and came trit-trotting up to the gates in a carriage like the ones Neetu and Sanjay had seen in films or pictures of Victorian England – and it was called a victoria. It was pulled by two smart horses – one brown, one white, with shiny leather and brass-embossed harness and each with a red feathered plume between its ears. The driver sat on a high seat at the front, the reins dangling between the fingers of one hand and a long, long whip in the other, with which to flick the horses into action.

First, Aunty Meena and Uncle Ashok carefully helped Great Grandma to the carriage and settled her in; then Grandpa held open the carriage door like a footman, and Neetu and Sanjay climbed inside and sank back into the red-leather seats.

So that they had plenty of room, Uncle Ashok said he and Aunty Meena would follow them on his motor-scooter.

The horses set off clip-clopping, their hooves echoing down the broad Calcutta streets. Neetu and Sanjay studied the old old lady who sat before them all wrapped up in her shawl. 'Is Great Grandma really going to bathe in the river?' they asked in puzzled voices.

'Oh, yes,' said Grandpa Chatterji. 'The river has become the most important place in her life.'

They stared out of the carriage windows as the horses trotted out into the road and joined a human river – a river of people who swept through that huge city, pulling things, pushing things, carrying things, – on their backs and on their heads; there were those who were riding on

bicycles, mopeds, in rickshaws or in trams and buses; it was a torrent of living creatures among which wandered dogs and pigs and horses and cows, where birds swooped and flapped and squawked and soared over the rooftops with the hundreds of fluttering paper kites.

Then Grandpa cried out, 'Look!'

They saw the huge, curving girders of a bridge which stretched over a wide expanse of shining water. It looked as though it had been built to carry the weight of the whole of mankind.

When they had crossed to the other side, they made their way along the river until they came to a place where many people had gathered.

The sunlight danced on the water, sparkling and shimmering. All sorts of boats and crafts floated like dreams through the liquid haze. Men, women and children stood at the water's edge, their garments fluttering. They bent and scooped water into their hands and rubbed their arms and faces, then they walked further into the river and finally dipped themselves under completely.

'This is where Great Grandma likes to bathe,' said Grandpa Chatterji, as the horses pulled up.

Neetu and Sanjay watched wonderingly, as Uncle Ashok and Aunty Meena led Great Grandma between them, down to the water's

edge. There, she removed her shawl and her slippers, put everything in a neat pile, and let out her hair. Uncle Ashok and Aunty Meena did the same then, each with an arm round Great Grandma to support her, they all entered the water and waded out until they stood waist-deep.

Garlands of marigolds and hollowed-out coconut shells floated around them as they cupped their hands and scooped water over their heads and drank and chanted prayers.

'But why do they need to go into the river to pray?' asked Neetu.

So Grandpa Chatterji told them.

'Once, many thousands of years ago, when the world was still being created, this river only flowed in heaven, high up beyond the highest peaks of the Himalayan mountains. The river was really the goddess Ganga, and her waters were so holy, that anyone who bathed in them would be cleansed of their sins and gain everlasting life.

There was a king living on earth – at a time when the world had only just been created and things were very new. This king had two wives, but no children, so he prayed devotedly to God and, at last, he was rewarded with the birth of many sons. The king was so happy that he looked for the finest horse in the land to sacrifice to God in gratitude.

At last he found the strongest, most beautiful, pure white horse and captured it, not realising that it belonged to Lord Indra. Before the horse could be sacrificed, Indra stole it back again. The king and his sons searched high and low for the horse, for they couldn't think of anything else that was good enough to offer to God. His sons even dug their way through to the centre of the earth looking for this horse. They dug so deep, that the goddess of the earth cried out in pain and her husband, Lord Vishnu, sent a terrible fire which burned the king's sons to death.

The king was grief-stricken. He hadn't meant to offend anybody and he begged God to bring his sons back to life. God told him, 'Your sons will come back to life when the River Ganga flows to earth.'

So now the king began years and years of praying and penance. At last, God was moved and allowed the goddess Ganga to flow to earth.

The river eagerly gathered herself together in a mighty torrent ready to plunge to earth, when Lord Shiva, the blue-throated one, the destroyer of evil, realised that the whole world would be destroyed by the river's force. As the heavens opened, he stood underneath and the great cataract thundered down on his head.

The great river was trapped in Shiva's tangled hair, and for a while, wandered over his head looking for ways to escape. Finally, she found seven partings in his hair and, breaking herself up, she was at last released from Shiva's head and flowed to earth, broken up into seven rivers. The pure mountain waters of the River Ganga tumbled down and with it came fish and turtles and porpoises and frogs and crocodiles and spray, which scattered like egrets. It was marvellous. Even the gods and angels and heavenly warriors, glistening with jewels, were amazed.

The rivers broke into streams and brooks and waterfalls and pools, and tumbled merrily down on to the arid plains, soaking deep into the earth. Trickles of it came to the ashes of the king's sons. As the waters mingled with their ashes, their souls came to life and ascended into heaven to live in happiness for ever.'

'So you see,' explained Grandpa Chatterji, 'the river Hooghly is one of those rivers and that is why people come to bathe here. They hope that when they die, their ashes will be put into the river so that their souls will go up to heaven.'

The children watched as Uncle Ashok and Aunty Meena helped Great Grandma to submerge herself completely in the water.

'Here, take these towels to them and a set of dry clothes to change into – and you can bathe too if you wish,' smiled Grandpa Chatterji.

'We didn't bring a change of clothes,' said Neetu in a disappointed voice.

'Oh, never mind. Go and bathe. Just take your shoes off,' said Grandpa.

'Can we really go in with all our clothes on?' cried Neetu and Sanjay with delight.

'The sun is so hot that if you run up and down for half an hour, you'll soon dry,' said Grandpa.

Neetu and Sanjay ran excitedly down to the water, but then both stopped before rushing in. They remembered Grandpa's story. This was no ordinary water. This river was holy. Sanjay took Neetu's hand, and feeling suddenly solemn, they stepped into the silky water.

'Look!' whispered Neetu pointing towards mid-river.

A great turtle seemed to swim specially close, so that they could see his shiny shell-back, his delicate but powerful arms and feet, and his smooth, gentle head, then he dived and disappeared from view.

Grandpa Chatterji watched his grandchildren with great contentment. He was glad that they had bathed in the waters of the Ganga before going back home to England.